The Vampire Upstairs

Written and illustrated by

Damian Woods

DEDICATION

Dedicated to the REAL Thomas and Natasha.

CONTENTS

ACKNOWLEDGMENTS

I would like to acknowledge the help, love and support of all my family and friends. They have helped and encouraged me throughout this whole process, and I will be forever grateful.

1. The HORROR!

THE YOUNG GIRL LAY IN bed, frozen to the spot.

Eyes wide with fear, staring at the figure in the doorway. The man, for that was its shape, was no man at all.

It was a Vampire.

Dressed in black from head to foot, the creature stared back at the frightened girl with glowing red eyes, blazing red like rubies. Red like blood.

It moved around the bed with almost no effort – floating, as if on air.

The girl still couldn't move. Nor could she scream, she was so paralyzed with fright. The creature knew. It stood over her like a pillar of night. It smiled its vampire smile, revealing sharp white teeth.

It sat next to her on the bed, still smiling.

Leaning towards her now, its mouth starting to open wide.

The girl began to whimper, but still no scream came.

The Vampire's mouth drew closer to her neck, the sharp teeth making dents in the soft flesh. And then... and then...

The TV screen went black.

"What the...?"

Thomas sat up, studying the screen, wondering what had happened.

Then he heard the *Voice of Doom*.

"That's enough of that rubbish," said Thomas's Mum.

He turned toward her. She was holding the TV remote like a trophy.

"It's not rubbish, Mum," he pleaded. "It's brill!"

"Well, let's just agree to disagree on that one, shall we?" she said, as she casually threw the remote on the couch. "Come into the kitchen a minute, love. There's something I need to talk to you about".

Mum turned and walked out of the living room. Thomas sighed and got up out of his chair, trudging along behind her.

Thomas Buckle was eleven years old. He had turned eleven in February and now it was July. The summer holidays had just begun but when it ended, he had to start BIG school. That's what his friends called it. BIG school. And he was much more scared of that than he was of the vampires, werewolves and mummies in the films he liked to watch.

He knew that.

And he also knew why his Mum didn't like him watching them. Because of Dad.

Thomas's Dad left when he was eight years old. He still didn't know why. He remembered his parents arguing a lot, mostly about money, but that was all. And because he didn't know for sure why Dad had left, Thomas sometimes blamed himself. And occasionally he blamed his Mum.

Mum worked very hard. She was a nurse and sometimes worked very long shifts. Sometimes she started early in the morning and sometimes she came home late at night. Being a nurse meant her hours were awkward and changeable. It was difficult for them to spend any quality time together. It was why he had been so close to his Dad. And why Mum and he were a little bit distant now.

Dad always seemed to be 'between jobs.' That was the phrase his Father liked to use. And Dad loved, loved, LOVED old movies. Especially science-fiction and horror. Anything from the nineteen-fifties and sixties. He had allowed Thomas to watch a lot of them, much to Mum's displeasure. Thomas had found some of them quite scary, but he enjoyed them none-the-less. 'Earth Vs the Flying Saucers' and 'Dracula Prince of Darkness' were among his favourites.

When Dad left, he didn't take any of his DVD collection with him, so Thomas watched them as often as he could. Mum didn't like that.

Thomas entered the kitchen.

2. The Kitchen

MUM WAS ALREADY SAT at the kitchen table with a cup of tea when Thomas walked in. He sat opposite her.

"Is something wrong?" he asked, worried.

"Not wrong, as such. But you might not like it" Mum replied.

"Okaaaay".

She shuffled in her seat. "The thing is, Thomas, we haven't really got a lot of money right now. There are lots of bills coming in and my job doesn't really pay that much so…" she trailed off.

"Do we have to move?" asked Thomas, worrying more now. He loved this house and a move probably meant a much smaller house or flat. And maybe even a different BIG school.

"No, no," she replied, hurriedly. "At least, not yet. What I'm planning on doing is getting a lodger."

Thomas hadn't really heard that word before.

"What's a lodger?"

"Well," said Mum, "it's like a house guest. Someone who comes to stay for a while but pays."

"Oh. So, we'd be like a hotel?"

Mum smiled. "Maybe more of a Bed and Breakfast than a hotel. I'm going to rent out the spare room. How do you feel about that?"

Thomas screwed his face up a little. He often did that when he was thinking.

"I'm not sure," he said, finally. "It doesn't really affect me much, does it?"

"Well it does," said Mum. "You might see this person more than I do, what with my shifts. I want you to be comfortable with it."

He still wasn't sure. But he felt more at ease with the idea, especially if it meant not moving to a new house.

"It'll be okay, I guess," was about as much enthusiasm as he could muster right then.

"We'll meet them together, of course," said Mum. "And I promise I won't rent out the room to anyone who seems a bit..."

"Weird?" added Thomas.

Mum laughed a little. He liked it when she laughed.

"Yeah. Weird".

She handed Thomas an envelope. "In there is the advert for the room and some money for the newsagent to put it up in their window. Would you go down there later and ask them to put it up for me?"

"Sure."

Suddenly, there was a knock at the door.

"It'll be Tash," said Thomas excitedly. "She said she was going to call for me today."

"Oh good," said Mum. "You can go to the shop together. There'll be some change left over. Why don't you get some sweets?"

3. Natasha

THOMAS LEFT THE KITCHEN in a bit of a hurry. He went to the bottom of the stairs and looked in the mirror that was on the wall. He checked his hair and had a general look at his face.

No dirt. No smudges. Good enough.

For some reason, Thomas always wanted to look good, or at least presentable, for Natasha (who preferred to be called Tash) but he didn't quite know why.

Thomas opened the front door.

Natasha was the same age as Thomas. And the same height. She was the sportiest person Thomas knew. Any sport available at school, Natasha played – and usually mastered in about an hour.

Thomas always thought she would make a fantastic wrestler, like the ones on the TV. She was really tough and any bully who dared try anything usually went away crying and cradling a part of themselves that was now very sore. He always thought she should be named after her own special move – The NUT-TAPPER.

Thomas looked her up and down. Her clothes were scuffed, as usual. Her hair was straggly and there seemed to be a twig tangled up in it. She had – as always – a huge smile on her face.

"Been climbing trees again?" asked Thomas, smiling right back.

"Yeah," said Natasha. "How did you know?"

"Oh, just good guess-work."

About two minutes later, Natasha and Thomas were walking down the street towards the local shops. Thomas had the envelope in his pocket. They had decided to get some fizzy cola bottles with the change. You're never too old for sweets.

"Did you hear the werewolves last night?" asked Natasha excitedly.

"Yeah, about half seven," he replied. "Like clock-work."

Thomas and Natasha had rather vivid imaginations, fuelled by the movies they both liked to watch at Thomas's house. At eleven years old, they were somewhere in the middle of still believing in the fantastical and the unknown but also realising a lot of it was probably rubbish.

Or, they were just a bit daft.

Take the werewolves howling, for instance. Neither child could quite put together that the sound of howling came from the same direction as the house where two Siberian huskies lived with their owner, Mr Cushing.

Had they the sense to ask, they would have found out that both huskies - called Fluffy and Sprinkles - began howling every time they heard the theme tune to Coronation Street, such was the pain.

And Mummies! They both believed in Mummies. How could they not? They saw one on a school trip to the History Museum. Okay, it wasn't moving, but who knows what happens after dark when the lights go out? And

Natasha totally swore she heard a sneeze coming from the Mummies glass case.

Thomas was also convinced that zombies existed. He was sure he'd seen those collecting trollies at the supermarket. Or was that in a movie? He couldn't be sure.

They didn't believe in aliens though. That was just stupid.

After putting the advert up in the newsagent window (and acquiring the necessary sweets), Thomas and Natasha ran to the park to play, chewing fizzy cola bottles and chatting about the monsters over-running the neighbourhood.

They hadn't met any vampires though.

Yet.

4. The Lodger

THOMAS'S MUM HAD A few days off. Instead of doing anything particularly interesting, she spent her time making the spare room look presentable for the prospective lodger.

Thomas didn't really help much. He carried a few things, moved a few boxes, but mostly played out with Tash or, time permitting, watched some more all-time classic sci-fi and horror movies.

Truth be told, by the time his Mums last day off came around Thomas had practically forgotten a lodger was even needed.

Then, one evening, there was a knock at the door. The sun had already dipped below the horizon and there was a strange purple haze in the sky. The air seemed heavy, somehow. Almost like a storm was brewing.

Mum looked at the clock on the wall. It was just gone seven pm.

"I wonder who that could be?" she said aloud.

Adults often say this aloud. Anytime someone knocks at the door or calls on the phone after six pm.

She went to answer the door.

Thomas sat with his iPad, doing some research on a cool old horror actor called Vincent Price. He wasn't really listening to Mums conversation at the front door. His ears did prick up a little when he heard Mum say "The room? Oh yes, it's still available. Please, come in."

It was about five minutes later, and Thomas realised he was still sitting alone in the living room. He got up and headed towards the kitchen, where he could hear two voices. One was his Mum, obviously.

The other he did not recognise. It was quite deep. Guttural even.

He walked into the kitchen to find his Mum sat at the table with a rather pale looking man. They both had cups of tea in front of them. His Mum took a sip out of hers. The man's tea stood untouched. The kitchen seemed very cold.

Mum noticed Thomas standing in the doorway.

"Oh, hello love," she said cheerfully. "Let me introduce you to Mr...?"

"Orlock" he said.

His voice was *very* deep, and there was a definite hint of an accent, even after hearing just one word. Especially around the 'r' sound. His name came out as *Orrrrlock.*

The man stood, holding out his hand for Thomas to shake. Thomas looked the man up and down. He was very tall. Over six feet. He had a dark goatee beard, which matched his equally dark clothes. His eyes were piercing.

Thomas took his hand and shook it. His grip was firm and icy to the touch.

"Nice to meet you," he purred.

"And you," said Thomas, glad to release the strange man's grip.

Mum had a fixed smile on her face and a faraway look in her eyes. "Mr Orlock is going to be our new lodger," she said.

"He is?" replied Thomas, confused. Mum had said they would meet and agree the new lodger together.

"I am verrrry pleased to be living here, Thomas. Your house is perrrfect for my needs." Orlock smiled briefly. His teeth looked sharp.

Thomas began to feel uncomfortable.

"I worrrk long hours. Nightshifts." The strange man smiled again.

"Do you mind if I just speak with my Mum a minute Mr..."

"Orrrrrlock," he said.

"Orlock," repeated Thomas.

Thomas guided his Mum into the hallway.

"What's the matter love?" she asked.

"The matter, Mum, is that you said we were going to pick the new lodger together, in case they were a bit... you know."

"A bit what?" she said, oblivious to any of the odd gestures Thomas was making with his head to indicate his thoughts that Orlock was a weirdo. He just had to come out and say it.

"A bit weird," he whispered, afraid Orlock might hear.

Mum's face suddenly took on a rather vague expression, as if she was recalling something from a long time ago. "Oh, don't be daft, love," she said blankly. Hypnotically. "Mr. Orlock is lovely."

All Thomas could do was roll his eyes. "How do you know he's lovely? You've only just met him."

"I just know. I took one look in his eyes and... and..." she drifted.

"And what?"

She shook her head, like shaking off a dream. "And I just know" she said.

A shadow seemed to descend between them then, as Orlock appeared in the doorway.

"Is everytheeeeng alright?" he asked.

"Of course it is," replied Mum happily.

Thomas looked on, bemused.

"Goooood. I will bring my luggage tomorrow eeevening" he said, silkily.

"I'm back at work tomorrow, Mr Orlock, but Thomas will be here to greet you in case I've not got back yet."

"That is veeeery good. I have only one large box."

"That's fine." Mum turned to Thomas. "That's fine, isn't it, Thomas?"

"Oh, yeah," he replied. A very strange, uncomfortable feeling was churning around his stomach. "Totally fine."

Outside, thunder rumbled.

5. Reflections

THAT WHOLE NIGHT AND ALL the next day, Thomas couldn't shake that strange feeling inside him. Orlock made him very uncomfortable, like he was wearing clothes that were too tight for him.

Even Natasha nut-tapping the local bully because he called her 'Tarzan' (she was climbing a tree at the time), couldn't shake him out of it.

Mum was due in about half seven. Thomas was hoping the strange new guest wouldn't arrive until after, but he wasn't that lucky.

At half six, there was a loud, deep knock. Then another. It was like the sound of dirt landing on a coffin-lid. (Bit dark that.) He walked half-heartedly out of the living room toward the front door.

He opened it with a smile on his face, trying his best to look pleased at the new lodger's arrival. "Good evening Mr..."

"Orrrrlock," he interrupted with a grin.

Thomas suspected that this oddball really enjoyed saying his own surname, given that he hadn't given him the chance to say it himself.

"Please come in," Thomas grinned back.

Standing beside Mr Orlock was a large wooden box. It was about a man's height and width, with rather ornate hinges. Brass maybe. An old family heirloom thought Thomas. Must be, if he's carting it around with him. Orlock could fit in that quite comfortably. He quickly pushed the thought from his mind.

"Would you like some help bringing that in, Mr Orlock?" he said aloud. Better start as he meant to go on. Didn't want to upset the man.

"That is veeery niiice of you to ask, young man," Orlock replied. "But I can manage."

Orlock lifted the box like it was made of air, effortlessly carrying it in. Thomas stared in awe at this incredible sight. Even the wood it's made of would be heavy, he thought, never mind the stuff that's in it.

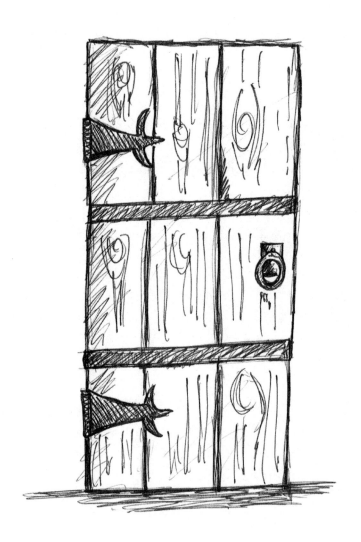

Orlock put it down in the hallway with a THUD.

Thomas closed the front door.

"Ummm, would you like a cup of tea?" (He couldn't think of anything else to say).

"No, thaaankyou. I never drink. Tea." Orlock smiled again, revealing a brief glimpse of those sharp teeth.

Maybe he's an all-night dentist, thought Thomas.

"I will take the box to my room, yes?"

"Uh, sure. You know where it is. Are you sure you don't need any help?"

"I can manaaage."

Orlock lifted the box again and began to carry it upstairs. Thomas had started to turn his head away, heading back towards the living room, when he suddenly did a double take. He saw himself in the mirror at the bottom of the stairs. And he saw the huge wooden box. He saw it being picked up. He saw it moving upstairs, with the little sideways motion as each foot goes up to the next step. He saw all this.

But he didn't see Orlock.

Had it been a second, he may have dismissed it as a trick of the light. But this was longer. About four seconds maybe.

Doesn't sound long does it? But count it for me now, out loud.

One.

Two.

Three.

Four.

Long enough to believe what you saw.

Or didn't see.

Suspicions began to form and grow right at that very moment.

6. Watching

THOMAS HAD ALWAYS THOUGHT the phrase 'watched them like a hawk' rather amusing. It suggested being perched on a tree with a strong pair of binoculars, arms folded like wings.

It wasn't as amusing now. He was desperate to catch another glimpse of Orlock in the downstairs mirror, though the rather sinister man wasn't giving him much chance. Thomas noticed that he just seemed to 'appear' during early evening, strangely, after the sun had faded away. And, more often than not, he would head straight to the kitchen, a tall, dark shadow in the doorway.

Thomas didn't know why Orlock avoided the living room. Perhaps he just didn't like children and had no desire whatsoever to interact with him.

Thomas didn't mind that at all.

He found Orlock to be a cold person – and not just to the touch. He was distant and didn't join in much conversation. Thomas had not learned any more about him since the day he arrived.

He did seem to hang around his Mother a lot, though. If she was back from work before Orlock had left for the night, he would speak to her briefly before leaving. Thomas could never hear what he said.

All of this odd behaviour was leading Thomas onto a particular train of thought. An odd, disturbing train of thought that, were he to say it out loud, would probably sound ridiculous. Even so.... all aboard.

7. Suspicious Minds

"SO, WHERE'S THIS WIERDO THEN?" said Natasha loudly.

"Shush!" replied Thomas quickly, dragging her through the front door and into the living room. "He might hear you. He's upstairs, sleeping."

Natasha slumped onto the couch. "Sleeping? It's two in the afternoon!"

"He works nights."

It was four days since Orlock had arrived. His routine thus far - sleep during the day, work during the night, had not altered. Natasha had been away at her Aunt and Uncle's caravan at the coast. It was probably as much holiday as she was going to get this summer, but she didn't mind.

Thomas had been keeping her up to date about the strange arrival with a daily text. He hadn't revealed his ultimate suspicions just yet, in case Natasha laughed at him. He needn't have worried.

He joined her on the couch.

"So, tell me everything," she said, seriously.

"Well, the first thing is, he's very pale. And cold. I shook his hand and it was really cold. Like ICE."

Natasha nodded. "What else?"

"I've not seen him eat anything, yet. He always says he's eaten but I don't know when. Unless he eats in his room."

"Mmmm," she mmmed.

Thomas thought for a moment, trying to get everything in order.

"He's really strong," he continued. "He picked up this HUGE wooden box like it was nothing. Light as a feather."

"Anything else?" she said, eagerly.

"Um, well, I don't know how to say this..."

"Come on!" Natasha said, excitedly.

Thomas braced himself for the inevitable backlash.

"Well, thing is, he doesn't have a reflection."

"What?!"

"I only saw for a moment and I haven't had a chance to look again, but when he passed the mirror, he wasn't reflected in it."

A long pause.

A loooooong pause.

Thomas waited expectedly.

"So," Natasha said, in her best summing up voice. "He doesn't appear during the day."

"Right."

"He's very strong."

"Yep."

She started counting the points off on her fingers.

"He's cold and pale."

"Uh-huh."

"You haven't seen him eat or drink?"

Thomas shook his head in the negative. "Not a thing."

"And he doesn't have a reflection?"

"Not that I've seen."

Another long pause.

"You're going to say I'm mad, aren't you? An idiot?" Thomas said worriedly.

"Nope," she replied with confidence. "I think you've got a vampire upstairs."

Thomas was filled with joy and relief that Natasha didn't think he was crazy. That was short-lived however, when he realised, he might actually have a real, live (well, un-dead) vampire upstairs.

Natasha broke into his thoughts. "What are we going to do?"

He noted the reassuring 'we'.

"Well, I'm going to have to really, truly make sure. I can't just go around blurting out that Orlock is a ... you know. Besides, what adult ever believes a child about stuff like this? And I'm not so sure about telling my Mum either. Tell you the truth, I'm a bit worried about her."

"Why?"

"She always behaves really weird around him. Like, distracted. She agrees with everything he says. It's like..."

"She's been hypnotised!" blurted Natasha.

"Yeah, exactly. He has her under his power."

Natasha scrunched her face up in thought. It was one of the many expressions she had that made Thomas feel like his cheeks were suddenly on fire.

"Well, you DO have to make sure," she said finally. "See if he likes garlic or not. That would be a good test. But not everyone likes garlic anyway, so you'd need something else. Have you got a cross?"

"I'm not sure. I think my Mum has one that my Dad gave to her."

"You could make one. Tape two pencils together or something." She made the shape with her fingers.

"I might ask my Mam to get a kebab tonight. With garlic sauce. She usually rings to ask what I fancy for tea. I could test the garlic out on him."

"Good idea," she nodded. "But be careful."

"I will" said Thomas, glowing inside.

"You know what we're really going to need though?" she said suddenly. "With werewolves, zombies and now vampires round here."

"What?" said Thomas.

"An estate agent."

They couldn't help but laugh.

8. Abra-kebab-ra

LATER THAT DAY, THOMAS'S Mum did indeed ring to ask him what he fancied for tea. She was planning to cook but agreed to the take-away. And so, at half six, Mum entered the house carrying the food.

Thomas followed her into the kitchen to help her unpack the takeaway (for reference, Mum had chicken nuggets).

"Where's Mr Orlock?" she asked.

Before he could answer, the man himself appeared in the kitchen doorway.

"Oh, hello" she said, surprisingly unsurprised by his sudden appearance. "Sorry I didn't get you anything. When I rang Thomas earlier you were still in bed."

"That is fiiiiine" he smiled. "I'm sure I will pick something up later."

In his mind, Thomas saw Orlock lick his lips at this point. He shook off the rather disturbing image and began unwrapping his kebab. He placed the carton on the table and opened it – seeing inside the small pot of garlic sauce.

"What do you like eating, Mr Orlock?" Mum asked.

Orlock smiled again. "I have a verrry... particular diet. Please, do not trouble yourself."

Mum sat with Thomas at the kitchen table. "Well, if there's anything I'm able to pick up for you, please let me know."

He bowed courteously. "Thaaaank you."

Thomas quietly peeled off the lid of the garlic sauce. He steeled himself for what he was about to do. He then asked, as innocently as he could, "Don't you even like garlic, Mr Orlock?"

He slid the little pot across the table towards the sinister man.

Orlock took an immediate step back, his eyes blazing. Thomas feared a sudden outburst (something he hadn't planned for), but it passed like a cloud.

"Pleeease" he said, "could you put that away. I have... allergies."

"Come on Thomas" said Mum. "Put the lid back on."

He did. Slowly.

"Sorry Mr Orlock" he said. "I didn't know people could be allergic to garlic." And now he decided to chance his arm even further. "Except vampires."

Orlock stared at Thomas. The stare was hard. "What imaginaaation you have."

"Must be all the old movies I like to watch," he replied innocently.

Orlock's eyes remained fixed upon the boy. "Perhaps. I must go now. My work is calling me."

They both heard the front door click closed as he left.

"What a lovely man he is" said Mum, digging into her chicken nuggets, her eyes strangely glazed over.

Thomas was worried. He was going to text Tash. After his kebab.

9. Don't box me in

THOMAS'S HEAD WAS SWIMMING. Orlock was a vampire. Orlock was a **VAMPIRE**.

At least, he thought he was.

But did he *really* know for sure?

There were plenty of reasons to explain a great deal of the man's strange behaviour. It's just, the most obvious one was 'un-dead'.

The morning after his trick with the garlic, Thomas found himself absolutely determined to find out one way or the other. Which could mean only one thing.

Going into Orlock's room.

He needed to see... what exactly? Thomas thought a lot about that. If he WAS a vampire, what would he see? Well, he wouldn't be in bed, that's for starters. He would be lying in the great wooden box, not snoozing between the sheets.

But then what? Open the box? Cross that bridge when I come to it, Thomas thought. He was up and dressed. He had heard Orlock enter the house earlier. And he had heard Mum go to work. It was about eight o'clock now. The sun was up and shining bright. Thomas steeled himself for the task ahead and opened his bedroom door.

There, not three feet away, was the door to the spare room. Orlock's room.

He stepped up to it and took hold of the door handle.

He stopped.

What if I am wrong, he thought? What if, when I walk into this room, he IS snoozing between the sheets and I wake him up? He's going to want to know why I'm there. Maybe I could say I was looking for something. Or ask him if he wants a cup of tea. Or water (he said he doesn't like tea, remember?) Hopefully he'd be too groggy to really take notice.

Okay then. All set.

He opened the door. Slowly.

And I mean slooooowly.

He stepped inside.

The first thing he noticed was the smell. A dusty, musty odour. The kind of smell you'd find in an attic full of cobwebs and mice.

Next was the darkness. The curtains were shut tight. They were a navy-blue colour, so as the light shone through, they gave the room the feel of midnight.

He peered through the gloom at the bed.

It was empty.

He stepped toward it and put his hand on it. He wasn't sure why, it just felt like he had to really make sure it was truly empty. It was. And there was a very thin layer of dust on the duvet. He could feel a slight grittiness beneath his palm.

The room wasn't very big, but in this strange darkness it felt like an abyss. He moved his head to the side to locate the box.

There it was.

He knew Orlock was in this room. He had HEARD him come into the house. There was nowhere else he could be.

Did he really NEED to look?

He stepped toward the box. His heart was pounding now. He felt like it would pound right out of his chest and knock on the box lid.

He knelt, his quivering fingers reaching out towards the lip of the wooden lid.

He lifted it. It gave a loud creeeak.

Thomas stopped what he was doing, holding the lid up just a few inches. He closed his eyes, fearing the grip of an icy hand suddenly shooting through the gap and closing round his wrist.

He opened his eyes and peered at his wrists.

Nothing.

The box lid was heavy. He lifted it a few more inches then looked into the darkness inside.

There seemed to be something pale, showing up against the blackness.

Thomas's eyes suddenly widened with terror. He recognised what it was. It was a hand, resting on what could only be Orlock's chest. His eyes looked upward a little further. In the dim light, he could just make out the shape of a chin and a nose. He was in their alright.

He was *IN THERE.*

The lid slipped out of his fingers with a smack of wood. Then he ran, out of Orlock's room (slamming the door behind him), down the stairs and out of the house. He hoped Natasha was at the Park so he could tell her the news.

10.Snooze-You-Lose

NO QUESTION NOW. THERE was a vampire upstairs.

Bizarrely, that night, Orlock mentioned nothing at all about Thomas's visit to his room. He had tried his best to avoid him but, inevitably, they had bumped into each-other as Thomas was re-entering the house. He had tried to stay out as long as possible, but as night drew in, staying out was just as dangerous an option as going home. He had made sure Natasha went home as well.

He had just gone through the door and immediately came face-to-face with Orlock, who merely bowed, said "Pleasant eeeeevening" and left.

Maybe he hadn't realised Thomas had been in his room. The 'vampire trance' had been too deep. Or maybe he DID know, and he was just pretending. Biding his time. Thomas thought he might go mad not knowing.

And so began a game of cat-and-mouse, with Orlock as the sneaky, evil cat and Thomas as the mouse. Though, thought Thomas, I'm more likely to be an asthmatic mouse. On crutches.

The following day, a report appeared in the local newspaper. (I know, children don't really read newspapers anymore – if ever – but both Thomas and Natasha were being extra vigilant for strange reports). This report was very strange indeed. And unpleasant.

Bodies found. Blood drained. Holes in the necks. (I could tell you more, dear reader, but it's all far too gruesome).

More evidence, if more where even needed, of Orlock's true nature.

Every new report that appeared, Thomas collected. Which would prove to be a mistake.

By the end of the week he had every newspaper report together in his room. He was sat on his bed, reading the latest piece of news - an unfortunate homeless man, drained dry like a carton of fruit juice. Suddenly, he felt a presence all around him and a feeling like an invisible band around his head. He rubbed his temples hard, trying to shake it off. Maybe I've been reading for too long, he thought. He glanced at his watch. It was quarter to seven.

In the evening.

"Interesting reading?"

Thomas turned toward the unmistakeable voice.

Orlock stood in the doorway.

Thomas looked down at his bed. All of the local papers were spread out on top of it. He gulped. "Um, yes."

Orlock stepped into the room and picked up one of the papers, hardly glancing at it. "Such a terrible thing, these deaths."

He sat on the edge of the bed.

"It would be such a shame, should anything like this happen to someone I know." Orlock looked pointedly at Thomas. "A young boy such as yourself should forget all about these horrors. They are not for young minds. Yesss?"

Thomas felt almost paralyzed. Orlock's eyes were boring into his. He felt as if he wanted to move – to run, to hide, anything – but his limbs would not obey.

"Yesss?" said Orlock again, more insistently this time.

"Yes," said Thomas. His brain would not allow him to say anything else.

"Goood." Orlock smiled. He stood up and moved towards the door. He was about to leave when suddenly he stopped and turned back toward Thomas. "And please remember, *my* room is *my* own." He left.

Thomas felt the invisible grip around his head disappear.

He let out a breath that he hadn't realised he was holding.

He was worried. He was scared.

He was more determined than ever to put a stop to Orlock's reign of terror.

But how?

11. Light in the Darkness

THE SUMMER HOLIDAYS DRAGGED ON.

Thomas was very careful not to mention or take notice of any more gruesome stories. Even his Mum, being a nurse, was aware of more bodies appearing in the hospital – blood drained, and all the rest of it. If she talked about it at all, Thomas was quick to change the subject in case Orlock was listening.

This would have two results, he thought. Not only would Orlock think Thomas was protecting his Mother from possible harm (which he was), Orlock would also think that Thomas was turning a blind eye to his vampire ways (which he wasn't).

The cat-and-mouse game continued.

Through it all, Thomas had started to have dreams.

Nightmares.

One of the most common nightmares is one where you are being chased. You're running as fast and as hard as you can, but your pursuer – whether it be a monster, a bully or just some dark, horrid *thing* gets ever closer, threatening at any moment to reach out and lay a bony hand, or sharp claw, on your shoulder. In Thomas's dream, he runs all the way through his own house until he reaches the foot of his stairs. He starts to run up them, toward an open doorway, with nothing but shadows beyond, when suddenly, a pair of red, gleaming eyes appear in the darkness. Thomas turns to run away, back down the stairs, but they turn into an awful escalator, pulling Thomas back and back and back, into the shadows and toward those blood-red eyes.

That's when he wakes up.

After having that nightmare three nights in a row, Thomas decided he had to come up with a plan.

12. Planning

ANY PLANNING THOMAS NOW did to try and stop Orlock would have to take place outside of his home. Natasha became his most trusted and eager helper. Any excuse to spend more time with her, really. Though vampire hunting wasn't exactly a first date activity.

They sat together on a bench in the park.

"What are we going to do?" she asked.

"There's only one thing we can do," replied Thomas, quietly. "We're going to have to destroy him, somehow."

He looked at Natasha. "No," he said suddenly "*I'M* going to have to destroy him. Me. I can't involve you in this."

The look of absolute disgust on Natasha's face at that moment could have shattered a thousand mirrors. "No way," she said firmly. "No way are you doing this on your own."

"But something really bad could happen to you. I can't have that." He looked into her eyes. He felt, at that moment, like giving her a kiss. Maybe just a peck on the cheek. He might have done it too, were he not afraid that she would break his nose if he tried. "You're my best friend," he said finally. That would have to do, for now. And he meant it.

"And you're my best friend, too," she replied. And she meant it.

Then they were all business again.

"Let's think about things for a minute," said Thomas. "What do we know about vampires?"

"That's easy. They don't like garlic".

"Right."

"Or crosses."

"That's an important one."

"Deffo," said Natasha. "But the biggest one has to be sunlight."

Thomas thought hard about that one. "Sunlight would totally destroy him. It always destroys Christopher Lee."

"Or there's always the stake through the heart!" Natasha exclaimed cheerfully.

"Tash!" said Thomas, horrified. "I may want him destroyed, but there's no way I'm stabbing him through the heart. I'm eleven years old!"

Natasha looked rather disappointed.

"Ok," she said, sadly. "So, what ARE we going to do?"

He came to one conclusion.

"Sunlight. Sunlight is the key."

13. The Long Game

THE PLAN WAS SET (kind of).

You will notice, dear Reader, that at no point has anyone decided to tell Mum. As those of you with any sense will know, telling adults about Vampires, Mummies and Werewolves being real, let alone in the local vicinity, let alone UPSTAIRS in the spare room, would be a complete and total waste of time. Plus, the strange hold Orlock had over her was potentially very worrying. Let us not mention it again.

It was the morning after Thomas and Natasha's planning session. Seven thirty. Early.

Mum had left for work. Orlock had come back into the house about an hour before. Thomas was awake all that time, listening to the comings and goings. When all was quiet, he got up and dressed.

First stop, Mum's room.

He tip-toed past Orlock's room. He wasn't sure why he did that, it just felt right. Once inside, he walked over to her dressing table, opening her jewellery box. Thomas felt slightly uncomfortable, rooting through his Mum's things, but it was all in a good cause.

Finally, he found what he was looking for. A gold necklace, with a gold crucifix hanging from it.

He was about to close the box when he noticed something else. It was his Mums wedding ring. He recognised it straight away. She had worn it for more than a year after his father had left. Thomas stared at it a while. He came to realise at that moment that he hadn't been particularly close to his Mum after Dad had walked out. She had tried so hard with him – worked long hours, tried to make sure he had everything he needed. So much effort.

How much effort had he put in with her, he wondered? That would have to change, he thought. If he managed to get through this.

He closed the box with a click and walked back to his room, putting the necklace under his pillow.

Next step – meeting Natasha at the park!

The sky was the brightest of blues, but the trees seemed to be full of crows. Black, hunched shapes, spying from the branches.

"This is it, then" she said, when he approached.

"Yep. Start of the endgame."

"Is it just that one thing we need to get from the newsagents?" she asked.

"Yeah. I hope they've got some" Thomas said. "This'll be a waste of time if they haven't."

They went on their way.

14. Panic Buying

THOMAS AND NATASHA SCOURED the shelves, looking for the one special item.

The Newsagent eyed them suspiciously. One child in the shop is bad enough. Two is cause for concern. Three or more is a sign of the apocalypse.

"Ah!" exclaimed Natasha. "Found it!"

The item bought and paid for, they both walked out of the shop. There was plenty of time to kill (no pun intended) and they decided to spend as much of it as possible outside in the sunlight, talking and playing. Trying to act 'normal', in the face of the bizarre, dangerous and yet somehow exciting task ahead.

They were back at the park, sitting idly on the swings.

"Do you think it's going to work, Tash?" asked Thomas. His confidence in the scheme was starting to diminish. He was thinking of how much of the plan – and their safety and the safety of his Mum, hung on the item they had just bought. It was currently in a plastic bag, hanging from his wrist.

"I think it'll work fine," Natasha said brightly. "We're going to do it together, remember?"

"It's going to be quite hard, keeping you at my house tonight."

"What do you mean?" she said, her nose wrinkling in confusion. "I'll just ask my Mum if I can stay over."

"And that's all right, is it?" he stuttered.

"Why wouldn't it be?"

Thomas shrugged. "Well, because I'm a boy and you're a... a girl, aren't you?"

She laughed. "So?" She punched him playfully on the arm. "Idiot."

He laughed back, feeling a little bit hurt. Both on the inside and from the throbbing pain in his arm.

"What are you going to tell your Mum?" asked Natasha.

"To be honest, I don't want her to know you're staying over."

"Why?"

"Well, if she knows, there's a chance Orlock will find out and I don't want him knowing you're there."

"Ahhh," she said, nodding. "You don't want him to know I'm your back-up."

"Exactly. And he comes back in the house about an hour before she gets up. I want it all over by then. So, you're just going to have to hide in my room, really quietly."

"That'll be a challenge." She laughed.

"I know."

They both laughed together, swaying gently back and forth on the swings.

15. Room with a View

THE HOURS PASSED. THOMAS and Natasha reluctantly made their way back to his house. As best they could, they avoided even glancing upstairs, toward the lair of the monster.

They watched a movie for a while, then Mum rang at five pm asking what Thomas wanted for tea. He asked her if Natasha could stay and eat with them. Mum happily agreed.

"She'll be in about seven," said Thomas. "Orlock will be up by then."

"Good."

"Good?!" he said, startled. "What's so good about it?"

"I've never seen a vampire before," she said eagerly.

Thomas shook his head in disbelief. Despite all the danger, she was still excited about seeing Orlock. Him? He couldn't wait to never see him again.

Half past six ticked round.

They heard the creak of a bedroom door opening.

Thomas turned to Natasha. "Careful what you wish for," he whispered.

The bedroom door closed with a thud.

Mere seconds later, the living room door opened. Thomas could feel a trickle of sweat rolling down his back.

Orlock entered. His eyes studied the room. They fell upon Natasha. He smiled. "Greetings" he said.

"Hello Mr Orlock" said Thomas nervously.

"Pleeease, introduce me to your frieeend."

Before Thomas could speak, Natasha jumped up and held her hand out. "I'm Natasha," she said, boldly.

Thomas thought he was going to faint.

Orlock took Natasha's hand and shook it. "Sooo very niiiice to meet you. It is such a pleasure to meet a friend of Thomas. You are a very pretty young lady."

Out of the three of them, only Thomas blushed at that.

"I am going to work now," Orlock lied. "Perhaps I can escort you home, Natasha?"

"She's staying for tea" said Thomas quickly.

Orlock turned his eyes on him. "I see. Another time then. But you must not stay out too late, Natasha. It may not be safe." He smiled at Thomas when he said that.

Orlock bowed to them both before leaving. When he had closed the door behind him, Thomas gasped out a breath.

"I can't believe you did that!" Thomas exclaimed. "Actually, spoke to him like that."

"No point making him suspicious," she shrugged. "Come on, let's plant that cross before your Mum gets in."

They walked upstairs and stood outside Orlock's room. "Here goes," said Thomas.

He opened the door.

They didn't turn on the light. Thomas didn't want Orlock seeing a sliver of light through the curtains – just in case he was outside right now, watching. They allowed the landing light to illuminate the interior of the room, however gloomily. It was as Thomas remembered.

They stepped inside.

Natasha took it all in eagerly. The cold, the musty smell. It all seemed to press down on them both.

Natasha couldn't help but let out a little shriek when she saw the box. She stepped forward and grabbed hold of the lid. Thomas grabbed hold of the other end and they lifted it up. All the legends said that a vampire slept in a bed of earth from its homeland. They weren't sure where that may be, but they knew it wasn't the Isle of Wight. They looked in.

Dirt.

"He really is a vampire" Natasha said.

Thomas looked at her in shock. "I thought you believed me from the start!"

She looked at him. "Well, I did but, you know. It's a vampire we're talking about here!"

He couldn't help but smile.

He reached into his pocket and pulled out the cross. He'd retrieved it from under his pillow earlier.

"All the movies are right so far. Let's hope this works." Thomas looked at the cross in his hand. He placed it in the box. It glinted in the dirt.

They replaced the lid.

16. The Last Supper

TEA AT THE KITCHEN table was a quiet affair. Mum asked them both about the day, asked about what they had both got up to. She was yawning before her cup of tea was even half-way finished.

"I'll wash up for you, Mum," said Thomas.

"And I'll help!" added Natasha.

"Awww, that's so sweet of you," Mum said, smiling. "I'll just go and have five minutes on the couch."

About two minutes after that, they both heard her snores drifting out of the living room.

The washing up lay finished on the draining board, the soapy bubbles oozing slowly down the plates and into the sink.

"Right," said Thomas. "You go and hide in my room. I'll be up in a few minutes."

"What about your Mum?"

"She'll be in bed by nine. Out like a light."

"I'll get bored waiting up there," Tash moaned.

Thomas rolled his eyes. "Just put the Xbox on. You'll need to make sure you've got headphones in, though."

"Alright."

She trudged upstairs.

Thomas stood over his Mum, watching her sleeping peacefully. "Things will get better soon, Mum," he whispered. "I promise."

She let out a snort like a pig. He smiled to himself and walked quietly upstairs.

17. Curtain Call

NATASHA LAY ON THOMAS'S bed, sleeping soundly. He sat in his chair in the corner, his old sleeping bag covering him. He was too on edge to sleep.

Mum had gone to bed about half nine. She had knocked quietly on his door to wish him goodnight. Tash had hidden in the wardrobe at that point, in case Mum had opened the door. Thomas had wanted desperately to fling his bedroom door open and hug his Mum tight but thought that would warn her something was amiss. Time enough for that later, he thought.

He hoped.

Sleep was washing over him now. His eyelids were drooping, his head was bobbing, until finally sleep took hold.

...

His mobile phone alarm vibrated in is hand, waking him instantly. Morning light was yet to bloom through the curtains. Orlock would be in any moment now.

"Tash?" he whispered.

"I'm awake." Her voice was strong. Focused.

He stood up. "I don't know what's going to happen, but I'm sure you'll know when to step in."

She slid off the bed and moved over to him. "I'll be ready."

Thomas had set a *particular* screensaver on his phone. He had it ready now.

They both heard the front door opening downstairs. Orlock stepped inside. There was a clicking sound as the door locked behind him. He began walking upstairs.

Thomas's heart was pounding so much, he thought Orlock was going to hear it.

He opened his bedroom door the tiniest amount.

The dark figure of the vampire came into view. Orlock opened his own door and stepped inside. He closed it behind him.

Thomas left his own room and waited. He thought for one ridiculous moment if Orlock had a bed-time routine. Maybe he cleaned his teeth first. Had a gargle of Listerine. He shook his head, trying to get the image out. He had to be ready. He wasn't quite sure what was going to happen when Orlock opened the lid of his box, but he knew it would be... noticeable. He clutched his phone tighter.

There was a feint sound of scraping wood. He was opening the box.

Any moment now, Thomas thought.

Suddenly there was a scream. A snarl of rage. Orlock had seen the cross lying in the dirt. His bedroom door flew open with such power, the hinges loosened.

Thomas saw him then, in all his horrific fury. Orlock's eyes blazed red. He saw Thomas in front of him, knowing then in that instant, that it was he – this *boy*, who had dared defile his resting place. He was about to strike, when Thomas lifted his phone – showing the picture to Orlock.

It was a picture of a cross.

The vampire cowered in fear and rage. Thomas moved forward pushing him back into his room. Orlock, knowing he was trapped, hissed and spat like a demonic cat.

Natasha was following. When able, she was going to slip by Thomas, armed with her own unique weapon, purchased from the newsagents and whip open the curtains. Hopefully, the sunlight would pour in and turn the creature to dust. There was just one problem.

The sun wasn't up yet.

"Brave children," snarled the vampire. "But children nonetheless".

Without any warning, Orlock flung himself out of the window. They could hear the tinkling of the glass as it hit the ground below.

"I wasn't expecting that," said Natasha flatly.

"Where's he going to go?" flapped Thomas. "He hasn't got time to hide."

"What's all that noise?" said Mum. All of the commotion had woken her. Any moment now and her bedroom door would open.

Thomas didn't know what to do. Everything was going wrong.

Suddenly, there was an almighty crash. Orlock had shattered the front door into splinters and was now thundering up the stairs, the violence of his movements totally silent, as his footfalls landed like air on the floor. He slapped the mobile phone out of Thomas's hand and grabbed him by the throat. He leaned in, his face only inches away from Thomas's. He could smell Orlocks's rank, evil breath as it swept over him.

"A good try, my young friend." He smiled, showing those sharp teeth. "But not good enough."

Then Mum opened her door. "What on earth...?"

She looked at the madness before her, trying somehow to put into words the jumble of thoughts going through her head. She got as far as "buh..."

Nobody could really think of what might come next.

Orlock snapped his head around to face her. His eyes bored into hers. "You are under my power" he said, his voice soft, yet dripping with venom.

"Yes," she replied, tonelessly. Her body had become rigid.

"Mum!" squealed Thomas desperately.

Orlock ignored him. "You will remove the cross from my resting place" he ordered her.

"Yes" she said again and walked robotically into his room, completely unable to resist the power of the vampire.

Orlock followed, dragging Thomas with him. Natasha could only watch, their plan in tatters.

Thomas's Mum had reached the great wooden box. She was about to lean over and pick up the necklace.

"Mum, please don't!" Thomas exclaimed.

"Silence!" hissed the vampire.

"Mum, I'm sorry."

She seemed to waver, just for an instant.

"Silence, boy!" Orlock hissed again.

"Mum, I'm sorry I haven't been that close to you since Dad left."

She stopped, still like a statue.

"Pick up the cross!" snarled Orlock.

"Mum..." said Thomas again. Tears had begun to roll down his cheeks. "I don't blame you for Dad leaving."

"You will do as I command!" shouted Orlock.

But Mum wasn't listening to Orlock anymore.

And the sun was rising.

"I love you Mum."

She blinked, as if waking from a dream. "I love you too," she said.

Natasha could see the sun rising. Before the vampire could find shelter elsewhere, she produced the squeezy bottle of Garlic Mayo bought from the newsagents. She squirted it around the door frame and at Orlock himself. He gagged at the smell, releasing his grip on Thomas's throat. Thomas ran to his Mum and held her tightly. Natasha joined them.

Orlock scurried round the room, like a rat in a trap. He had nowhere to go. The garlic acted like a pungent force-field, preventing the creature from leaving.

And the sun rose.

He glared at Thomas, red eyes bulging with hate and fear. The sunlight hit him like a wave, instantly turning him into dust. It floated on the breeze that came in through the shattered window.

"It's over," said Thomas. He looked up at his Mother's face.

She looked confused and concerned, the influence of the vampire gone.

"Why can I smell garlic?" she asked.

18. Ever After

THE SUMMER HOLIDAYS were over and Big School beckoned.

After Orlock ended up as something to grit the path with, his strange hold over Thomas's Mum faded away. She couldn't remember much of anything about his time in the house and was convinced he was a 'scoundrel' (her words) and 'up to no good'. The story she had constructed in her head was that Thomas and Natasha had caught Orlock trying to rob the house and did a tremendous amount of damage.

Neither Thomas nor Natasha dispelled her theory.

Thomas and his Mum found themselves bonding anew over the house repairs. Painting and tidying. They found themselves hugging more and laughing easily around each-other. And they were both happy.

Mum had mentioned, with money still being tight, that they might have to move somewhere smaller. She assured him that she wouldn't move out of the area and that he wouldn't have to move school.

Both confident and content, he awoke on his first day of Big School with a light heart.

Until he saw the building.

It was huge.

HUGE.

He stood at the school gate, staring up at the building, his heart sinking ever so slightly as pupils, much older and taller, passed either side of him like twigs in a stream.

"Hey!"

He turned toward the familiar voice, smiling as he saw Tash running toward him.

"Hi," he said, a little bashful. (She looked very pretty this morning.)

They both looked up at the building.

"Big, innit?" she said.

"Yep. It's scarier in person than it is in the leaflet," he replied.

Thomas suddenly felt her hand take his, squeezing it tightly. His face turned a little red, but he looked at her and smiled.

"We'll face it together though, right?" said Natasha, beaming at him.

"Yeah," he smiled back. "Together."

They walked through the gate.

The End

ABOUT THE AUTHOR

A passionate reader from being very young, Damian has always enjoyed being transported to other worlds and into fantastical situations by books of every kind – horror, science fiction, adventure and fantasy. A playwright for more than ten years, Damian has published fourteen plays and short sketches. He is also the author of The Cowardly Knight and Wicked Ways, both books for children, a book of poems called A Little Nonsense, plus Dracula Reborn and Dracula's Legacy, both sequels to the original classic novel. All are available on Amazon.

Printed in Great Britain
by Amazon

82674345R00047